MY BROTHER IS A
ROBOT

BOOK 5

THE DISCOVERY

AMANDA RONAN

TOWN AND COUNTRY
PUBLIC LIBRARY DISTRICT
320 E. NORTH STREET
ELBURN, IL 60119

The Discovery
My Brother is a Robot #5

Scobre Educational
2255 Calle Clara
La Jolla, CA 92037

Scobre Operations & Administration
42982 Osgood Road
Fremont, CA 94539

www.scobre.com
info@scobre.com

Scobre Educational publications may be purchased for
educational, business, or sales promotional use.

Cover and layout design by Nicole Ramsay
Copyedited by Kristin Russo

ISBN: 978-1-62920-507-6 (Library Bound)
ISBN: 978-1-62920-506-9 (eBook)

For Bethany—my almost-twin sister.

CHAPTER 1

"**O**KAY, ANY QUESTIONS ABOUT THE SCIENCE FAIR?" MR. Denny shouted over the noise of the class bell. "No? Well, you know where to find me!"

I hurried out into the hallway to meet up with my best friend, James, before our next class. James had borrowed my math book that morning to do his homework during study hall and I wanted to get it back before class. We had a quiz on factoring equations and I'd studied a lot. I actually felt ready for the test, which had never happened to me in math before, so I wanted to look through the book one more time, just to be sure.

James wasn't waiting for me at my locker like we'd planned. I started looking around anxiously and checking my watch every five seconds.

"What's wrong, Shawn? Don't tell me you're nervous about the math quiz. You're more than ready," my twin brother Cyrus said, walking up to me from the science lab. We had a few classes together, but didn't hang out too much at school. Cyrus was a popular jock and I was a normal, invisible sixth grader.

I shrugged. "Thanks again for helping me study last night. I just want to get my book from James so I can go over everything one more time."

Cyrus shook his head. "You'll be fine. I mean, after all, your private tutor is a genius robot that knows just about everything there is to know and just happens to be an expert in sixth grade math." He smiled and waited for me to acknowledge how he'd just praised himself.

See, Cyrus was my twin brother, but he wasn't my brother by blood. He was my brother by science. My mom is an engineer and created the world's most lifelike robot. After she'd perfected the circuitry, she didn't really have time to worry about what the outside looked like, so she had the artists at her lab make the robot look just like me. Yep, she handed them a family photo and told them to replicate me. Clearly she didn't think that decision through!

Mom brought Cyrus home just about one year ago in order to help him perfect his human-like qualities and learn emotional reactions. I immediately saw the value of having a robot brother, so I had Cyrus do my schoolwork for me, which got me kicked off the basketball team. This made my dad upset, and even though it was my fault, he blamed Cyrus. He also didn't like all of Cyrus's programming glitches like his alarms going off in the middle of the night, and he wanted my mom to bring Cyrus back to the lab. Cyrus wanted to get on my dad's good side, so he learned all about the things my dad liked and planned a whole kitchen remodel to build my dad the cooking space of his dreams. Unfortunately, the remodel didn't go too smoothly and my dad freaked out when he saw the house torn apart. Eventually, though, the two of them rebuilt the kitchen together and bonded in the process.

Once my dad and Cyrus started getting along, it seemed like things would finally settle down for our family. Sadly, that didn't happen. I had to miss a basketball game, after finally getting back on the team, and Cyrus agreed to cover for me. One of Mom's colleagues at the lab discovered that Cyrus was pretending to be me and revealed our switch to the whole town. People got upset that the lab was making robots who would impersonate humans and that might lead to robots doing bad things and people getting blamed. The lab was considering ending Mom and Cyrus's program, until my friends and I launched a social media campaign showing the world how amazing Cyrus was. When a video of Cyrus saving a little kid trapped in a skee-ball machine went viral, the lab let Cyrus stay with us permanently. Mom and Dad adopted Cyrus and he became my brother.

After all that drama, we went away for the summer and had a great time at my grandparents' lake cabin. When we got back home, Cyrus and I started sixth grade and the drama came back. Cyrus was really popular with the older kids, who knew all about his robot skills and wanted to use him to win soccer games and ace their homework. I had an unfortunate incident with pizza in the cafeteria and got called "Pizza Boy" by everyone at school. I also failed to make the basketball team. I felt really bad about myself and took it out on Cyrus by picking a fight with him in the hallway a few months ago. We talked it out with the school counselor and since then things have been good. Cyrus spent most of his time with his new friends, which was okay with me, because I was busy trying to keep my grades up. I also didn't want to draw too much attention to myself; I don't need another horrible nickname.

I rolled my eyes at Cyrus. "Yes, oh great one, you are a master at all things sixth grade. How many times do I need to thank you for helping me study?"

Cyrus smiled. "A few more times couldn't hurt."

I saw James running down the hall towards us with my book in his hand. He was soaking wet. "Sorry, man. My study hall is in the portable building, and it's raining so hard that the campus is flooding." James shook his head like a wet dog, spraying water everywhere.

Cyrus tilted his head. He was making his "checking available databases" face. Then he blinked and said, "That hurricane they were predicting veered off course, it looks like it might hit us harder than expected."

I wanted to stay and hear more, but I had to run to math class. I grabbed the book from James and just made it in the room when the bell rang. As I closed the door behind me, Cyrus was still standing in the hallway contemplating the news of the hurricane. I found my seat and opened my book, hoping to get in a few seconds of cramming before the test started.

Cyrus didn't show up to lunch. I asked all around and no one had seen him since science. After lunch, I went to English class and starting working on a group project with James and Demarcus.

"Mrs. Jasper, please send Shawn Cole to the office. His mother is here to get him," the secretary announced over the intercom.

Mrs. Jasper handed me the homework assignment for the weekend and wrote me a hall pass. I wondered what my mom was doing at school. She usually worked long hours. My dad worked part-time from home, so he was usually the one to come to school when needed. I got a knot in my stomach worrying that something had happened to Cyrus and that was why he wasn't at lunch. I started walking faster, not wanting to wait any longer to find out.

My mom was waiting in the office. Rain dripped from her hair onto the carpet. She was holding an umbrella, which was also soaked.

"Mom?" I asked, "did something happen to Cyrus?"

She turned to the school secretary to thank her and then wrapped a wet arm around me. "No, he's fine. He called your dad earlier to pick him up. The two of them are out buying supplies for the house. The hurricane winds are going to start within the next few hours. It's going to be a bad storm this weekend."

"But, all the other kids are still here at school. Shouldn't they be going home, too?" I asked, worrying about my friends.

"Attention, all students! This is your principal Mr. Sprell. The National Weather Service has just advised the county to begin hurricane preparations. You'll be dismissed early today. Teachers, please release students to the busses at the end of this class period."

The principal made the announcement just as Mom and I were walking out the front door.

"See," she said, "nothing to worry about."

CHAPTER 2

DAD AND **C**YRUS GOT HOME FROM THE GROCERY STORE AND hardware store not long after Mom and I got home from school. The rain continued to beat down and the winds picked up speed as we unloaded Dad's car. Our basset hound, Scooter, stood in the open door and howled. He did not like storms.

"Mom, my network connection keeps dropping off," Cyrus said when we all got inside.

"It's probably just the storm. Download any updates

you need and email status reports to me now, in case something important goes offline."

"Is Cyrus going to be okay?" I asked Mom as we walked into the kitchen.

"Yep, in fact he should be ready to get to work in just a minute." Mom smiled, trying to reassure me.

Mom asked Cyrus and me to work inside the house while she and Dad closed the shutters over the windows outside.

I lifted one of the bags from the hardware store onto the kitchen table and peered inside. "Why do we need so much duct tape?" I pulled out three gray rolls and set them on the table.

"Duct tape is very handy. You can use it to fix broken windows and seal drafty doors. You can wrap strands of it together to make a rope. You can make a sling for a broken arm with it, too. Oh, and you can make indestructible wallets out of it," Cyrus laughed, grabbing the tape. "It was in the survival section of the hardware store, so we tossed it in the cart."

"Where should I put all this stuff?" I looked down at the millions of packages of batteries, the first aid kit, and the beef jerky.

Cyrus looked up from the floor where he was busy filling coolers with ice. "Put everything in the closet in Mom's office. That's where we'll go if the storm gets really bad, like if the windows start breaking."

"I thought that was just in case of a tornado?" I asked, lifting up the bags to bring them into the office.

Cyrus shrugged. "It's both. The wind during a hurricane can be strong enough to uproot trees and pick up anything not securely attached to the ground. Mom's office will be the safest place because it doesn't have any windows."

Scooter followed close at my heels as I opened the door to Mom's office. The room was a mess with papers and machinery everywhere. I looked down at

Scooter and asked, "How are we all going to fit in here?"

Scooter whined a little and cowered near the door. I kneeled down to scratch his ears and tell him it was going to be okay.

Behind me, I heard my parents come in the front door. They'd finished clearing the yard of anything that might get picked up by the wind and closing the shutters over the windows. Both of them were soaking wet, their rain coats having done nothing to keep them dry.

"Oh good, you're starting on the office," Mom said. "Just put all the papers in one corner. You can unplug all the machines; I backed up all the files earlier today. Sorry it's such a mess, champ. I'm going to help Cyrus organize the food and water."

I cleaned up Mom's office as best as I could and made some room in the closet for the hurricane supplies. When I was finished, I went to look for Scooter's memory foam doggy bed in the living room. I wanted to be sure to put it in Mom's office so Scooter would be comfortable in case we got stuck in there. I found my dad sitting on the couch. He was hunched over the coffee table scribbling a note on the back of a magazine. On the television, the newscaster was going through a list of things to have with you during a hurricane.

"Dad?" I squinted, trying to make out his notes.

"Shhh!" He hushed me and tried to keep up with the list. In a few more minutes he sat back on the couch and looked at me. "Sorry, son, I didn't mean to shush you, I was just trying to make sure we're ready."

That made me worried. I thought my Dad knew how to take care of everything, but seeing him panic a little about this hurricane made me think that maybe he didn't have everything under control. I knew that meant I needed to step up. "What else needs to be done? What's on the list?"

My dad wrapped an arm around my shoulders and squeezed. "We've got plenty of water and food that won't spoil. Go find the hand-held can opener, and then gather the extra pillows and blankets from the upstairs closet and put them all in Mom's office. I'm going to go outside to look for our sleeping bags in the shed."

Once we had all the supplies organized, it was late in the evening. Dad decided to make burgers and a salad for dinner. We ate in front of the television, watching the news report on the hurricane as it continued to make its way close to land.

"Well, at least we still have power." Mom smiled as Cyrus collected the dirty plates. It was his turn to do dishes, and even though there was a raging storm outside, my dad wouldn't let us get out of our chores.

"Don't jinx us, Samira." My dad smiled at her.

And then the lights went out.

The wind howled outside our windows all night. After dinner we tried our best to play a few board games by candlelight, but every time the house creaked, we all looked around nervously.

"Maybe we should go to bed early. It's dark enough," my mom suggested, looking tired from all her worrying.

I felt too amped up to go to sleep. "I have to finish my book for school. Can I stay out here with a flashlight and read?"

"Me, too?" Cyrus asked.

Mom nodded and went into the office.

"We'll lay out the blankets and sleeping bags so you boys are closer to the door. Don't forget to bring Scooter in with you. Don't stay up too late," Dad warned. "It will be a long day of clean up tomorrow when the storm stops."

When Dad closed the office door behind him, Cyrus patted the sofa cushion next to him. Scooter happily hopped on the couch and snuggled with Cyrus under a quilted blanket.

I laughed, "Don't let Dad catch you inviting Scooter on the couch. He'll be angry!" I heard Scooter sigh under the blanket and knew he'd be snoring gently in just a few seconds. I leaned back in the recliner and pulled my knees closer to my body. It wasn't cold in the house, but I felt chilly. The constant sound of rain outside didn't help. I aimed the flashlight at my copy of *Hatchet* and picked up reading where I'd left off.

"It's weird, isn't it? Reading a book about survival while we're trying to survive this hurricane," Cyrus said, putting his book down. He wasn't using a flashlight because his photo-optic robot eyes could see in the dark.

"I wouldn't say we're trying to survive. I mean, we've got it pretty good here with a house and plenty of food and water. We'll be fine. It's not like we're questioning our well-being day to day, like some people in the world have to. Now, can I get back to the book? It's just getting good." I turned the page.

"What do you mean, like some people in the world have to?" Cyrus asked, sitting up and disturbing Scooter's sleep enough to make him bark once.

"Use your databases and look it up. People in this world live without enough food and drinkable water. There are terrible diseases without cures. There are people with no homes. All we have to put up with is a little rain." I smiled to myself, finally feeling like I knew something Cyrus didn't. When my brother got quiet I knew he was trying to search for information online. "So—?" I asked waiting for him to tell me what he'd discovered.

"The network is down," Cyrus said suddenly. "Give me some examples that I can look up when things are up and running. I think I'll do some research tonight."

"Research about what?" I asked.

"About human survival," he said, waiting impatiently. He didn't like relying on me for information.

I shrugged, "You could look up the Dust Bowl, or malaria, or water contamination, drought, famine . . . I dunno, Cy. There are just so many people in the world who live in really terrible situations. I wouldn't know where to tell you to start."

Cyrus got quiet and then whispered, "With the rain."

I listened to the rain beat down on the house and garage and the lawn, but I didn't know what Cyrus was talking about.

Finally he spoke again and laughed, "Without access to all that information, I'm just a like a real human."

I looked at him over the top of my book and said, "Except for your flashlight eyeballs."

Cyrus laughed and said, "You got me there." He picked up Scooter and went into Mom's office. I sat in the living room for a little while and listened to the storm howl outside. Morning couldn't come soon enough.

CHAPTER 3

IT RAINED THE NEXT DAY, BUT THE HEAVY WINDS HAD DIED DOWN enough for us to get outside and inspect the house for damage. A few tiles had flown off the roof, and some of the trees in the backyard had lost a few branches. We felt very lucky that our family was safe and our home had not been destroyed. Power was restored by Sunday, and we found out about the severe damage in other parts of town. The elementary school had flooded when part of the roof collapsed. The rest of the schools in town had leaky roofs, and there was water damage in many classrooms. In order to let everything dry out and to make sure there wasn't an unhealthy amount of mold, the district canceled classes for the week.

"So, what do you want to do this week?" Mom asked over dinner. "I could take some time off and we could go somewhere together."

My dad cleared his throat and looked at Cyrus, then he said, "Actually, Cyrus and I are going away for a few days."

My mom coughed in surprise. Scooter scampered over to sit near her feet hoping that food might fall off the table. Though he'd been scared, Scooter had done okay during the hurricane. He'd curled up in the space between Cyrus's sleeping bag and mine. After taking a sip of water, Mom asked, "What do you mean? Where are you going?"

"I'm taking Cyrus on a survival camping trip up in the Redbridge Mountains. We'll probably be gone three nights," my dad explained.

I looked back and forth between my parents, who obviously hadn't discussed this plan yet. Cyrus also seemed interested in how my mom would react. Though he was adopted, he was technically still her work project.

Mom folded her hands on the table, pushing her dinner plate away and asked, "A survival trip? Why? And why isn't Shawn going?"

I shook my head quickly from side to side. "No way, I don't want to live out in the wilderness for four days with nothing but a shoelace and a canteen. No *way* would I go!"

My dad laughed, "Well, that's why Shawn isn't going. I didn't think he'd want to. Remember that time we sent him to overnight camp? He called us crying the first night because the mattress was lumpy."

I shrugged. "I don't like roughing it. I want a comfortable bed with a pillow top mattress, if possible. I'm not ashamed of that."

"Mom." Cyrus turned to her. "The night of the hurricane, Shawn told me about people all over the world surviving in difficult environments. It got me curious about all the things I didn't know about human life and survival. I asked Dad some questions about survival stories and he offered to take me on a camping trip. It's all for research."

Mom nodded slowly. "I see. You're curious about people who live a different life than we've provided. I think it's a great idea. What a wonderful experience!"

Dad and Cyrus exhaled a little, glad Mom hadn't said no.

"Just make sure you keep a detailed record of your experiences. We'll want to log the data and add it to robot programming in the future." Mom smiled and looked at me. "Okay sport, it's just going to be you and me. What do you want to do?"

I used my fork to push the pieces of corn around on

my plate and said, "I don't know. Maybe you can help me with my science fair project?"

Mom's eyes went wide. "Really? You want me to help? Oh my goodness, Shawn, we're going to have such a good time putting something together. In fact, I'm going to go start brainstorming some ideas!" She pushed her chair out and went into her lab.

My dad chuckled, "Uh oh, you're in for it now. She's not going to give up until you come up with a way to stop global warming."

My dad was right. When it came to science, my mom was crazy. I laid my forehead on the table and moaned, "What have I done?"

James and I were playing basketball at the hoop in front of my house. Dad and Cyrus had been gone two days and Mom had spent a lot of time at work, but kept dropping hints about her ideas for the science fair.

"Foul!" James cried. "Are you even paying

attention? You just slapped me across the face. Keep your eyes on the ball, Cole!"

Since James had made the basketball team, one of the few sixth graders who did, we barely hung out after school. I had to shoot hoops by myself. I was a little rusty at playing with someone else. "Sorry," I said, and watched him easily sink two shots from the foul line.

"You want to come over and watch TV? I'm getting hungry," James said.

I was about to take him up on it when my mom's car turned down our street and she honked the horn excitedly at me. As she pulled up and unrolled the window, she had a huge smile on her face. "Ready to work on the science fair project? I brought some stuff home from the lab!"

James watched my mom pull into the driveway and shook his head at me. He said, "That's cheating. Your mom is a mechanical engineer. She can't help you with the science fair project. You'll make the rest of us look bad."

"Why?" I asked, "What are you making?"

"Probably a clay volcano," James laughed. "I'll see you tomorrow!" He turned and jogged up the driveway in front of his house.

I helped my mom carry boxes into the house. Once we were in her office, I started unpacking them. "What are we going to do with all this stuff?" I looked around at the wires, motherboards, pipe cleaners, glue, and sheets of metal.

My mom grinned and rubbed her hands together. "Whatever you want! But I was thinking you could design a program to predict the flu virus, you know, more than just a year in advance like they do now."

"But, Mom—" I started.

She held up her hand, "Okay, okay. I know. You want to do something cool. What about a floating skateboard? Like a hover board. All you need are a few . . . " she went on to list a bunch of materials that were completely foreign to me.

"Mom," I finally interrupted, "what about something easy and normal? Like a volcano or a pulley system?"

Mom sighed and looked around the room at all the gadgets she'd brought home. "Too much?"

I nodded. "Yeah, I think maybe a little. But Cyrus has to do a project, too, so maybe he'll want some of this stuff."

My mom looked reassured by that. "I'm sorry. I shouldn't have pushed this on you. I just thought it would be something fun we could do together."

I walked across the room and hugged her. "It's cool, Mom. I really appreciate you wanting to help."

She smiled, "You know what else could be fun to do together? Go get pizza."

She didn't have to ask me twice!

CHAPTER 4

DAD AND CYRUS GOT HOME LATE SUNDAY NIGHT. I WAS getting ready for bed when I heard the car pull in the driveway.

"They're home!" Mom shouted from downstairs.

Scooter's ears perked up and he joined me as I ran down the steps. I was really excited to hear about their adventure. I couldn't say that I actually liked camping, but I knew how much it meant to my dad and Cyrus, so I wanted to hear all about it.

Cyrus opened the front door and quickly walked

through the living room, not even stopping to pet Scooter, who was nipping playfully at his feet.

"Hey, man. How was it?" I asked, following Cyrus through the door and into the kitchen.

He was looking around in one of the drawers where we kept odds and ends. "Do you know where the flashlight is? I thought I put it back here after the storm."

I looked over his shoulder and shrugged. "Nope. Maybe it's still in Mom's office?"

Cyrus turned around and walked out of the kitchen without saying another word. When the door to the kitchen swung open again, it was Dad.

"Hey, what's with Cyrus?" I asked, hugging him.

My dad shook his head. "I have no idea. He was like that the whole way home. Totally silent. Once we got back into Wi-Fi range he's been running all kinds of searches and scribbling notes on his tablet." Dad opened the fridge. "Yum. Is that mushroom anchovy pizza for me?"

I wrinkled my nose. "Of course. No one else in the family eats pizza covered in fungus and smelly fish."

Dad chuckled and grabbed a slice of cold pizza. "Just the way I like it. That way I don't have to share!"

Mom walked in and smiled. "I see you found your dinner. What kept you so late? I thought you'd be home earlier?"

Dad nodded, "I did, too, but every time we came across something new—every plant, every animal noise—Cyrus wanted to record it, take photographic evidence of it. He was just so into nature I couldn't make him leave."

"Well, the boys have school tomorrow. Hopefully Cyrus can recharge quickly tonight. I'm excited to see what data he's captured in that last few days." She looked around. "Wait? Where is Cyrus?"

A banging sound outside made us jump. Dad

peeked out the kitchen window into the back yard and said, "Looks like he's in my work shed."

"What's he doing in there?" Mom wondered aloud. She opened the backdoor and called, "Cyrus, what are you up to?"

"Just trying something out. I got an idea while we were camping and I want to see if it will work," Cyrus called back.

Mom, Dad and I went out to the shed and saw Cyrus sketching something on the tablet that was built into his palm. They looked like blueprints.

"Cool. Is that your science fair project?" I asked walking behind him.

Cyrus turned around quickly and hid the work he'd been doing. "Um, no. I mean, yes. That's why I don't want you to see it."

I looked back at my parents and they just shrugged. Cyrus was always weird. I mean he was a robot after all, but this took weird to a whole new level. "Well, okay," I said, backing up. "I'll let you work on it, then. I'm going to bed."

Cyrus didn't even look up at me.

"Oh, to be fair, Mom brought a bunch of stuff home from the lab for me to use for my science fair project. So if you want to use any of it—" I started to say.

Cyrus looked at Mom. "You did?"

She nodded and he ran out of the work shed.

I turned to my parents looking for some sort of explanation of my brother's bizarre behavior. "What was that all about?" I asked.

"I have no idea," Dad laughed.

Mom seemed less amused. "It's like he's discovered something and he's not ready to share it. That's very unusual for him."

"Well, he's an unusual guy," I laughed. I said goodnight to my family and motioned for Scooter to follow me to bed. As we walked by the office, I heard

Cyrus going through all of the things Mom had brought home.

As we reached the top of the stairs, both Scooter and I were startled by a sudden, "Ah-ha!" from below.

"Guess he found what he was looking for, huh boy?" I asked Scooter, who just looked at me sleepily and curled up on the end of my bed for a good night's sleep.

"Hey, Pizza Boy!"

I frowned and peeked around my locker to see Rodney coming down the hallway. On the first day of school, I had tried to help James at lunch and ended up getting four pieces of pizza smooshed into my white shirt. After a couple of months, it seemed like people had forgotten about the "Pizza Boy" nickname. Of course, Cyrus's eighth grade soccer buddy, Rodney, had no trouble reminding everyone as he hollered it down the crowded hall.

"Hey, Rodney," I said slamming my locker shut.

"When's your brother coming back to school?" Rodney asked, not returning my greeting.

It had been two weeks since Cyrus and Dad returned from the survival camping trip. Since then, Cyrus had been working nonstop in the shed, which he'd turned into his own personal lab. He received packages from mail-order science companies everyday. When I did see him, which was rare, he barely said anything to me. I had tried joking with him about not overachieving on the science fair project, but he didn't get the joke. He just said that whatever he was working on wasn't for the science fair and went back to the shed.

Though Cyrus was technically a robot, he was enrolled as a student at our middle school. Mom was the only person Cyrus let into the shed. Once she learned what he was working on, she arranged for the school to send his work home with me. So every day I had to collect his assignments and bring them home.

At home, Cyrus would finish his homework in fifteen minutes, while it took me over two hours. It wasn't hard to be jealous of my robot brother.

I started making my way down the hall toward my next class and shrugged at Rodney. "I dunno. He's working on something big, so maybe not for a while."

"What about the soccer game tomorrow?" Rodney yelled after me. "We need him at center. Jeremiah isn't as good as Cyrus!"

Without turning around I held up my hands to let him know it was his problem. He'd only wanted Cyrus on the team to help them win games with his special robotic powers, anyway. Now Rodney would have to figure it out.

As I walked through the door to my math class, I felt myself get pulled back into the hallway. Rodney was gripping the strap on my backpack and frowning. "I'm serious, Cole. We need your brother at midfield.

The Rams are scared knowing that they have to face a robot and it's going to help us win."

I shook myself free from his grasp. "What do you want me to do about it?"

"Pretend to be your brother, at least on the sidelines, to keep them scared," Rodney said.

I shook my head, "No way, man. Been there, done that. We don't trade places."

Rodney crossed his arms, "Fine, then at least join our team for the game, so we have enough players. You don't have to pretend to be Cyrus. After all, it's not like you're busy with the basketball team."

Now I was mad. I stood up taller and looked Rodney right in the eyes. "Being a jerk is not going to get you what you want. Soccer is Cyrus's thing, not mine. I'm not interested in your little offer. My brother will be back eventually. Just be patient." I turned around and walked into class without waiting for Rodney's response.

CHAPTER 5

"**V**ERY NICE PROTOTYPE, SHAWN," MY SCIENCE TEACHER, Mr. Denny, said as he stopped by my display at the science fair. "Tell me, what gave you the idea to make a basketball slingshot?"

I held up the y-shaped plastic tubing with the large exercise band strung between the two prongs. "Well, we've been studying force and motion, and I love basketball, so I wondered if I could make something that could be related to both. I tried different materials for the slingshot to see which helped make the most shots from the free throw line. It was actually a really fun experiment."

Mr. Denny smiled and nodded. "The mark of a great inventor is someone who has fun while creating new tools for the world. You've got a great future ahead of you in science. Thinking of following in your mother's footsteps?"

I laughed and shook my head. "No, sir. I'll leave that to Cyrus."

Later in the evening, my slingshot was awarded "Most Innovative." I couldn't wait to get home to show Mom and Cyrus my ribbon.

In the car, my Dad kept telling me how proud he was of my accomplishment. It felt great, like I was finally the smart one in the family.

When we got home Mom was sitting on the couch with Cyrus. In front of them was something that looked like a blender.

"Are you here to congratulate me with a celebratory

milkshake?" I pulled out my award ribbon. "Because I actually won something at the science fair!" I did a little dance around the living room and sang, "Go Shawn, it's your birthday . . . " until I noticed no one else was joining in.

"That's really wonderful, honey," Mom said.

Dad stood next to me, beaming. "We've got two smart kids, honey. Shawn's science teacher spoke very highly of him when he presented the award."

"Nice job, Shawn!" Cyrus said. "What was it that you invented? I've been so wrapped up in my own project I never asked you about yours."

I shrugged and grinned. "A basketball slingshot . . . only the most life-changing device ever."

Mom smiled and then patted the seat next to her. "Actually, that reminds me. We have some family business to discuss."

I pointed at the blender and frowned. "So, no milkshakes?"

She shook her head. "Not right now, no. Maybe tomorrow, though, okay? We will definitely celebrate your success soon."

My dad looked as puzzled as I felt. He sat on the loveseat and clasped his hands together. "Okay Samira, tell us what this is all about, because I can't handle the suspense."

My mom looked at Cyrus and nodded. "I'll let Cyrus tell you."

Cyrus pointed to the blender and said, "I created a two-part hydrogen, one-part oxygen soil extractor."

My dad and I looked at Mom for translation.

"What Cyrus is saying is that he built a machine that can create water from dirt, rocks, sand, and soil," Mom explained.

My dad leaned forward and examined the machine on the table. "So, it's like a juicer for rocks?"

Cyrus nodded. "Kind of like that, yes."

"And the water is clean? Drinkable?" My dad peered over at Cyrus.

My brother nodded again.

I watched as my mom and dad exchanged the "What do we do now?" glance back and forth. I was still confused. "So what's the big deal?"

"The big deal," my mom said, "is that this machine can take resources like sand and dirt that are found in places where rain is scarce, and turn them into water. It has the potential to save hundreds of thousands of lives."

"Not to mention how it could be used during emergencies. Remember during the hurricane how we had to buy all that water? It was because if the town water gets contaminated or the generators don't run to filter the water, it becomes undrinkable. This is small enough that every family in the world could own one and not worry about thirst or dehydration ever again," my dad added.

I nodded. "Oh, so it's a pretty cool invention then. Why didn't you enter it in the science fair?"

Cyrus said, "I just finished it tonight. It would not have been ready in time. Besides, it probably would have won an award and then people would have thought the science fair was rigged, with us both winning."

I laughed, "Good point." I knew Cyrus was kidding, but it felt good to joke around. I'd barely seen him in weeks.

"So, what do we do with it now?" Dad asked. "I mean, is it property of the lab since Cyrus created it?"

My mom sighed and looked worried. "I'm torn. Part of me knows we have to bring it to the lab. They do technically own it and we can't keep this technology from the world. It's too important. But the other part of me knows that if we go public with this," she looked over at Cyrus, "we may lose Cyrus."

I felt like I'd been punched in the stomach. "What

do you mean?" I stood angrily. "They can't take him away for experimenting. He didn't do anything wrong!"

"No, Shawn, not take him away in a bad way, take him away to work on more devices or to do press for the lab. He'd become an instant celebrity, a worldwide hero," my mom explained.

I sat back down, "Oh. Well, then, I think we should keep it here. No one has to know."

"Shawn, I can't keep this from people. It will help humans everywhere. You're the reason I built it. I mean, you inspired me to learn more about human survival. In fact, I named the machine after you," Cyrus said.

"You did? What is it? The Awesomenator 1000? Coolbro X? StylinShawn 5000?"

Cyrus laughed, "Calm down. No, it's the 3SN for Shawn, Samira, Scooter, and Nathaniel."

My mom wiped a tear away and my dad coughed like he was trying not to cry.

I nodded. "That's amazing, bro. I love it. But, what about the 3SNC, for Shawn, Samira, Scooter, Nathaniel, and Cyrus?"

Cyrus smiled. "Yep. That's perfect."